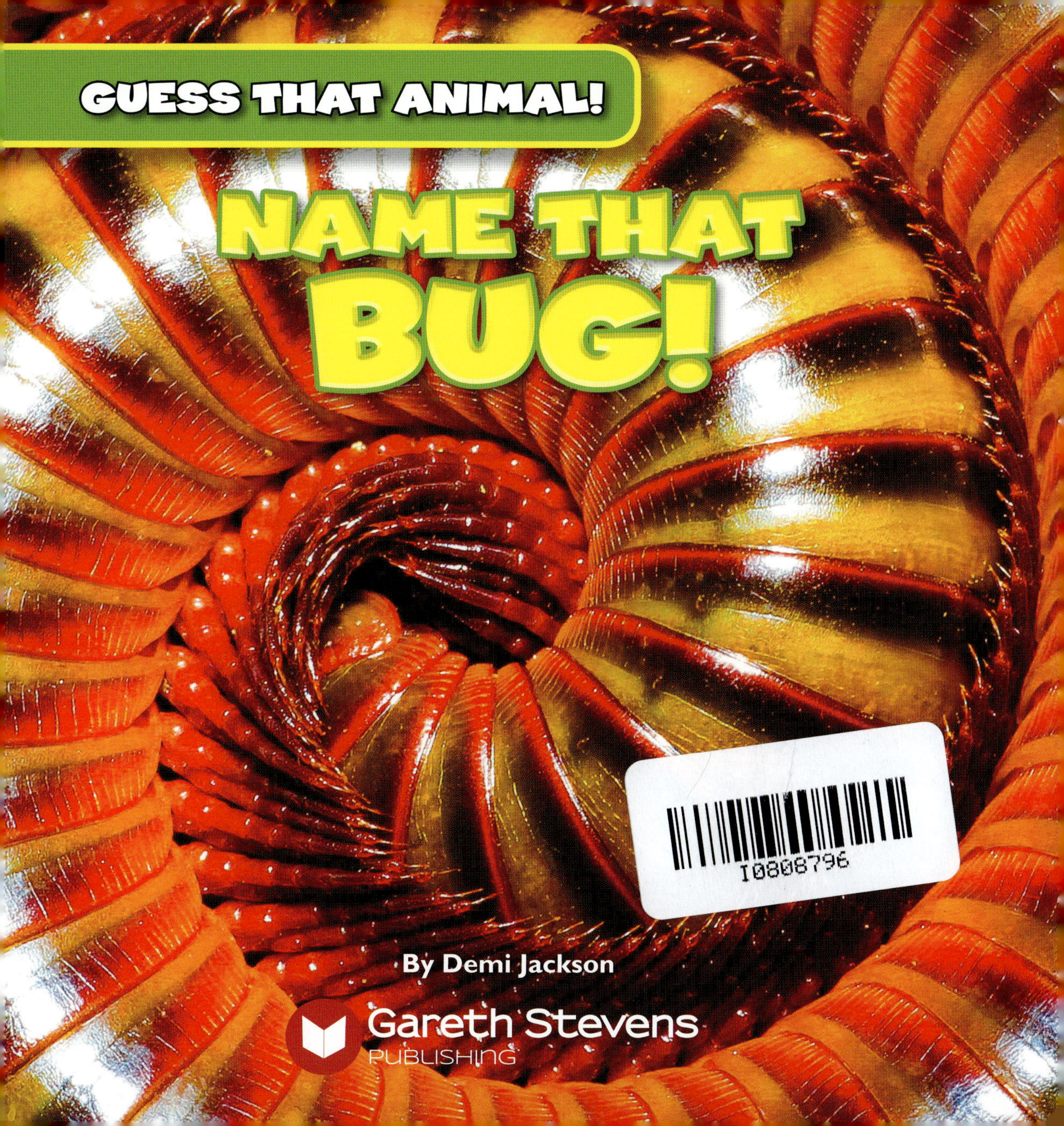

GUESS THAT ANIMAL!

NAME THAT BUG!

By Demi Jackson

Gareth Stevens
PUBLISHING

Please visit our website, www.garethstevens.com. For a free color catalog of all our high-quality books, call toll free 1-800-542-2595 or fax 1-877-542-2596.

Library of Congress Cataloging-in-Publication Data

Names: Jackson, Demi, author.
Title: Name that bug! / Demi Jackson.
Description: New York : Gareth Stevens Publishing, [2017] | Series: Guess that animal! | Includes bibliographical references and index.
Identifiers: LCCN 2016003830 | ISBN 9781482447514 (pbk.) | ISBN 9781482447446 (library bound) | ISBN 9781482447026 (6 pack)
Subjects: LCSH: Insects–Juvenile literature.
Classification: LCC QL467.2 .J327 2017 | DDC 595.7–dc23
LC record available at http://lccn.loc.gov/2016003830

Published in 2017 by
Gareth Stevens Publishing
111 East 14th Street, Suite 349
New York, NY 10003

Designer: Andrea Davison-Bartolotta
Editor: Kristen Nelson

Photo credits: Cover, p. 1 Khritthithat Weerasirirut/Shutterstock.com; p. 5 Richard Whitcombe/Shutterstock.com; pp. 7, 9 saied shahin kiya/Shutterstock.com; pp. 11, 13 RusticBoy/Shutterstock.com; pp. 15, 17 Sari ONeal/Shutterstock.com; pp. 19, 21 Ron Rowan Photography/Shutterstock.com.

Printed in the United States of America

CPSIA compliance information: Batch #CS16GS: For further information contact Gareth Stevens, New York, New York at 1-800-542-2595.

CONTENTS

Boldface words appear in the glossary.

What's a Bug?

There are billions of bugs on Earth! "Bug" is the word used for insects, spiders, and other small animals that look like them. Insects are animals with a three-part body and six legs! Can you name any of these bugs ?

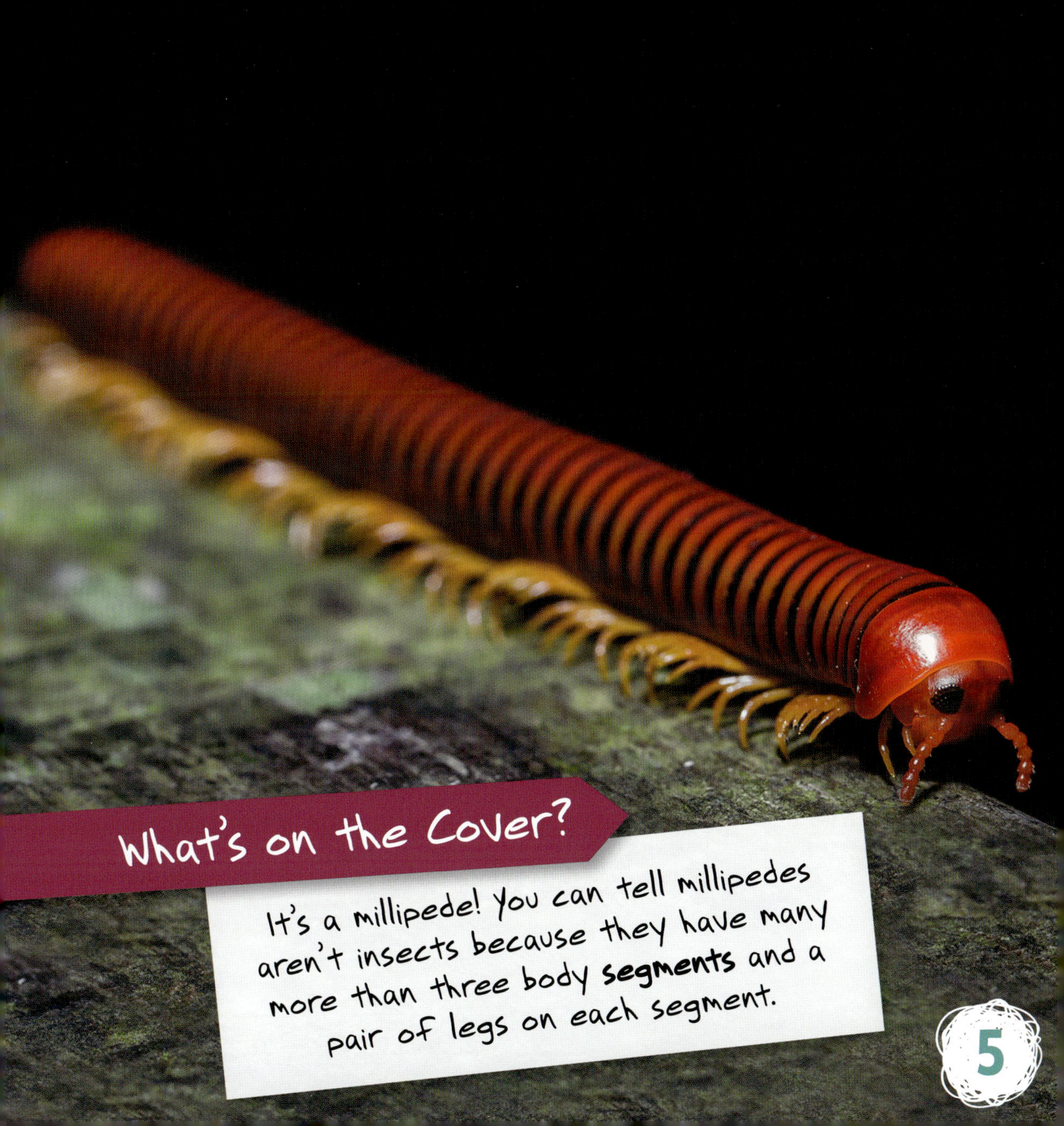

What's on the Cover?

It's a millipede! You can tell millipedes aren't insects because they have many more than three body **segments** and a pair of legs on each segment.

Lady in Red

This bug is known for its bright red color and black spots. It's small and has short legs. Like many bugs, it has antennae, which are body parts that help animals sense the world around them. What is it?

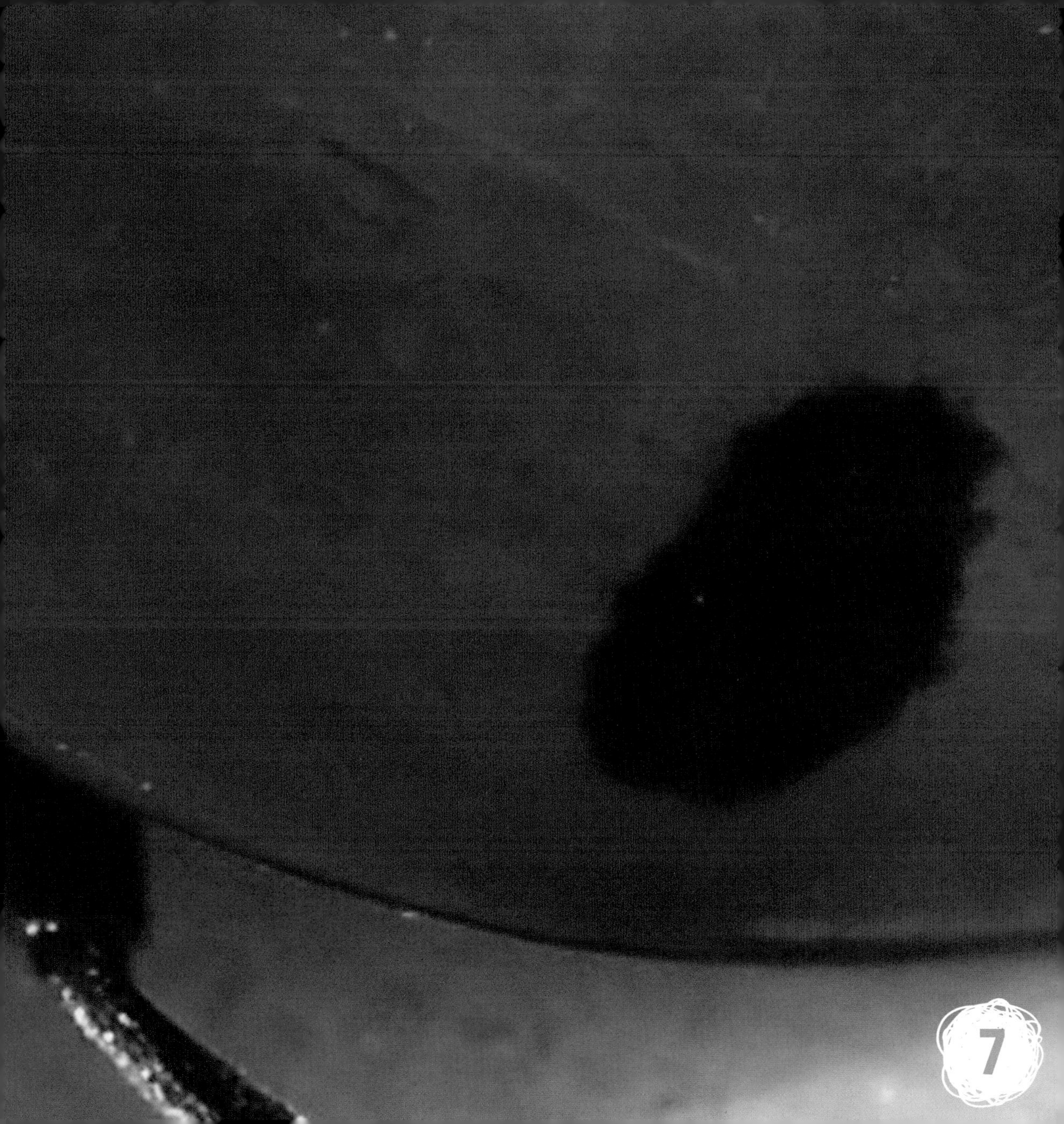

It's a ladybug! Ladybugs are a bright color to let predators know they taste bad. There are about 5,000 species, or kinds, of ladybugs. Most ladybugs eat plant-eating pests, so farmers love them. But a few eat plants, and farmers don't like them!

Hardworking Bug

It's easy to tell this bug is an insect. It has a large head and a narrow area between its other two body parts. This bug is known for being strong, and it has strong **jaws**, too. What is it?

It's an ant! Like most insects, ants **hatch** from eggs. The queen ant may lay thousands of eggs! Ants live in big groups, which may be found in trees or underground.

Beautiful Flyer

Many insects have wings, but this bug's are more noticeable than most! After hatching, this bug's larva is called a caterpillar. It makes a **chrysalis** when it's ready to grow into an adult. Can you name the bug?

It's a butterfly! The monarch butterfly shown here is common in North and South America. You can spot monarchs by their orange-yellow and black wings. Like the ladybug, these colors tell predators they aren't good to eat!

More Legs

There are more than 43,000 kinds of this bug. They all have eight legs and a two-part body. Many are small and don't bother people. But some are larger and **poisonous**! What kind of bug is it?

It's a spider! You might spot this black-and-yellow garden spider in your yard or at the park. Like other spiders, garden spiders build webs in which they catch food and may lay their eggs.

GLOSSARY

chrysalis: the case around the pupa of an insect as it grows

hatch: to break open or come out of

jaws: the walls of the mouth

poisonous: having poison, which is something that causes illness or death

segment: a part of an insect's body

FOR MORE INFORMATION

BOOKS

Hengel, Katherine. *Cool Birds & Bugs: Great Things to Do in the Great Outdoors.* Minneapolis, MN: Checkerboard Animal Library, 2016.

Murray, Laura K. *Ants.* Mankato, MN: Creative Education/ Creative Paperbacks, 2016.

WEBSITES

Bugs
animals.nationalgeographic.com/animals/bugs/
Do you love bugs? Find pictures and information on the National Geographic website.

Fun Insect Facts for Kids
sciencekids.co.nz/sciencefacts/animals/insect.html
Read many interesting facts about bugs!

INDEX

leveled reader
science

GUESS THAT ANIMAL!

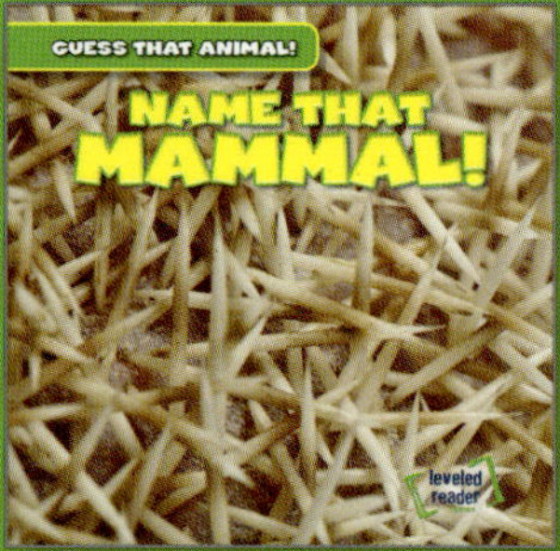

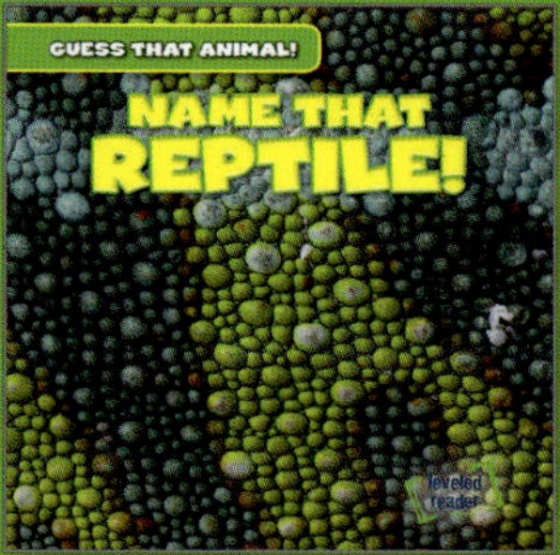

Levels: GR: H; DRA: 14

ISBN: 978-1-4824-4751-4
6-pack ISBN: 978-1-4824-4702-6
9 781482 447514

Gareth Stevens
PUBLISHING

BIOMAS DONDE YO VIVO

VIVO CERCA DE UN DESIERTO

Lecturas graduadas

Walter LaPlante